Sir Gadabout
Gets Worse

Also by Martyn Beardsley

Sir Gadabout
Sir Gadabout Does His Best
Sir Gadabout and the Ghost
Sir Gadabout Goes Barking Mad

Find out more about **Sir Gadabout** at
http://mysite.wanadoo-members.co.uk/gadabout

Martyn Beardsley

* * * * * * * * * * * *

Sir Gadabout

Gets Worse

Illustrated by Tony Ross

Orion
Children's Books

For Sarah and David Carlyle

First published in Great Britain in 1993
by Dent Children's Books
First published in paperback in 1994
Reissued in 2006 by Orion Children's Books
a division of the Orion Publishing Group Ltd
Orion House
5 Upper St Martin's Lane
London WC2H 9EA

1 3 5 7 9 10 8 6 4 2

A catalogue record for this book
is available from the British Library

Printed in Great Britain by Clays Ltd, St Ives plc

ISBN-13 978 1 85881 054 6
ISBN-10 1 85881 054 X

The Orion Publishing Group's policy is to use papers that are natural,
renewable and recyclable products and made from wood grown in sustainable
forests. The logging and manufacturing processes are expected to conform to
the environmental regulations of the country of origin.

www.orionbooks.co.uk

Contents

·1·

A Very Important Guest

A long, long time ago, when there were no video recorders and you had to decide whether to watch the football match and miss the James Bond film, or watch the film and miss the football, there lived a knight called Sir Gadabout.

He sat at the famous Round Table in the majestic castle of Camelot, a place so remote that even the paperboy had a job finding it. Sir Gadabout was a loyal subject of noble King Arthur and his Queen, Guinivere – the sight of whom made all men's hearts flutter. Aside from her beauty and the fact that she was as good at woodwork as any man, Guinivere had recently patented a cure for hiccups, involving the use of a knitting needle, a snorkel, and a pound of strawberry jelly.

The King and Queen were such fair and wise rulers, and so loved by their subjects, that there was very little lawlessness in the land. In fact, Sir Lancelot, the Greatest Knight in the Whole World, and all the other knights of the Round Table, were reduced to jostling each other in a rather ungentlemanly fashion in order to be first to fight any marauding dragon that happened to stumble into the Kingdom.

Sir Gadabout tended not to fare too well at these times. Compared to the other knights, he was not quite so strong nor as fast, as nimble, as clever as ... anything, really. Despite this it was not so long ago that he had rescued Guinivere from the horrid witches Morag and Demelza. It had taken a certain amount of luck, it is true, but everyone seemed to have forgotten about that now. All Sir Gadabout had achieved since then was to accidentally pole-vault out of the arena on his spear during

a joust, and take on a "dragon" – which had turned out to be a slightly oversized Dutch Limping Toad. Needless to say, he had lost the fight.

One day, just after lunch, a guard brought King Arthur news of visitors at the main gates.

"Who is it?" asked the king.

"It is Sir Rudyard the Rancid and party, your Majesty," said the guard.

"I can't say I've heard of him. Are we expecting visitors today?"

"No, your Majesty. However, he says he is a knight in the service of King Meliodas of Lyonnesse."

"Is he indeed?" mused King Arthur. Meliodas was a famous ruler and a friend of his. "Then we had better meet Sir Rudyard the Rancid." He turned to Sir Lancelot. "I think I ought to send Sir Tristram along to greet him."

"He's gone on holiday, your Majesty."

"Then Sir Bors can do it."

"He sustained a broken leg in his valiant attempt to assist Lady Eleanor, your Majesty."

"I'd forgotten. Sir Mordred?"

"He's had to wait in for the gas man."

There was a long silence as King Arthur tried to think of someone else who could greet his visitors.

At that very moment, Sir Gadabout walked by . . .

Sir Gadabout was hard-working and kind-hearted, but he was not what you might call the "better class of knight". In fact, he was officially the Worst Knight in the World. He was tall and thin; his suit of armour always seemed too big for him, and his sword was broken in the middle and fixed with sticky tape. It had nevertheless helped him through numerous disastrous quests, as indeed had Herbert, his faithful squire who accompanied Sir Gadabout everywhere. Herbert was a short, stocky young man with straight brown

hair almost covering his eyes. He was devoted to his master and had been in many a fight with those who dared to insult Sir Gadabout.

It was Sir Gadabout who got the job of meeting the visitors. He accompanied the guard to the massive castle gates. The heavy wooden drawbridge was lowered over the moat, and Sir Rudyard the Rancid and his party clip-clopped across on their horses.

"Greetings. I am Sir Gadabout, and I wel-come you to Camelot."

"Well met, sir knight. I am Sir Rudyard the Rancid, loyal Knight of King Meliodas of Lyonnesse."

Sir Rudyard was so big and fat that his poor horse seemed to be sagging at the knees. His puce-coloured armour had built-in bulges to accommodate his bloated belly, his many chins and various other prominent parts of his vast body.

His shield was emblazoned with a crest made up of a plate piled high with bangers and mash, though since the shield was rarely cleaned, the food looked well past its sell-by date.

When Sir Rudyard opened his mouth to speak, Sir Gadabout noticed that it was full of black and browny-yellow coloured teeth, and Sir Rudyard had the unfortunate habit of spitting whenever he said a word with the letter *s* in it. His podgy face reminded Sir Gadabout of an enormous potato with a squashed nose and two little piggy-eyes.

"This is my wife, Lady Belladonna," said Sir Rudyard the Rancid, introducing a thin-faced woman with a pointed nose and chin and a poisonous glare. "And this is my squire, Ivan Tussler." Ivan Tussler was at least seven foot two, with arms like tree trunks and an almost square, shaven head.

"Last, but not least," said Sir Rudyard, "is my little doggy, Michael, who is affectionately known as Mad Mick."

The dog, a black, flea-bitten thing, trotted up to Sir Gadabout wagging its tail, and rolled over playfully on its back.

"Aah!" said Sir Gadabout, bending down to tickle its tummy. "What a lovely – OUCH!"

Mad Mick sank his teeth into the knight's hand.

"You startled him!" accused Lady Bella-donna in a shrill voice, as the dog trotted back to his master wearing what looked like a smug smile.

"My apologies," said Sir Gadabout diplomatically, dripping blood over the courtyard. "What brings you to Camelot, Sir Rudyard?"

"We come as humble travellers, lost in the treacherous mists surrounding Camelot, seeking refuge from fellow knights whose generosity is famed throughout the land."

"That wretched paperboy sent us the wrong way," said Lady Belladonna venomously.

"Now take me to King Arthur, there's a good lad," said Sir Rudyard.

"Very shortly," said Sir Gadabout. "My squire will take care of your horses while I see if the King is ready to receive you."

In the meantime, King Arthur had been

preparing to meet his distinguished guest. He had put on his royal robes and crown, and he and Queen Guinivere moved to the throne room where they always met visiting dignitaries.

"What's this visit all about, Gads?" asked the King, as he settled himself into the diamond-studded throne, his famous sword – Excalibur – by his side.

"They're seeking temporary refuge here, your Majesty. They got lost on the way back to Lincoln West."

"Lyonnesse," hissed Herbert, who was good at geography and could name every capital city in Europe and parts of the Far East.

"We never turn anyone away from the gates of Camelot – send him in," declared King Arthur.

Sir Gadabout and Herbert went to summon Sir Rudyard for an audience with the King. "King Meliodas is a very great ruler with an army of knights almost as famous as those of the Round Table," Sir Gadabout told Herbert as they went.

"Sir Rudyard the Rancid doesn't strike me as a champion knight," remarked Herbert. "And they don't look very lost, either. There's something fishy going on, if you ask me."

However, Sir Gadabout always liked to see the good side of people; he ignored his squire's remarks and took the visitors to see King Arthur.

"Your Majesty, allow me to introduce Sir Rudyard the Rancid of ... of ... Lyme Regis."

"Lyonnesse!" whispered Herbert resignedly.

Sir Gadabout started again. "Allow me to introduce Sir Rudyard the Rancid of Lyonnesse, his wife, Lady Belladonna, and his squire, Ivan Tussler. Oh, and his dog, Michael."

"Known affectionately as Mad Mick," added Sir Rudyard.

"It's a pleasure to meet you," said King Arthur. "Any knight of my friend King

Meliodas is welcome here. And what a cute little doggy!"

The dog scampered gaily up to the King, who leaned down to pat him. Without warning, Mad Mick flicked his head round and nipped Arthur on the nose.

"You made a sudden movement!" complained Lady Belladonna bitterly in her high-pitched voice. "You scared poor Michael."

"How thoughtless of me," replied King Arthur tactfully as he felt his throbbing nose for damage.

But Sir Rudyard was eyeing the King's magnificent sword. "And that must be the famous Excalibur?"

"It is indeed." King Arthur proudly patted its bejewelled hilt.

"They say," said Sir Rudyard, "that it is priceless – that it even has magic powers."

"There may be some truth in that," agreed the King. "But you must be tired and hungry after your long journey. Rest now, and this evening we shall have a fine feast in honour of your visit."

"You are even more generous than I had heard," said Sir Rudyard, adding, "It will surely be a special and serendipitous start to our stay to sit and sup at your side." (Which was unfortunate bearing in mind his habit of

spitting when he pronounced the letter s.)
King Arthur was too polite to wipe his face
until they had gone. He ordered Herbert to
take them to the guest rooms.

Herbert guided the visitors up the stairs to
the large and well-furnished quarters. On the

way, Mad Mick tried to take a chunk out of Herbert's ankle when no one was looking, but the squire, already suspicious of the new-comers, hopped out of the way just in time. Lady Belladonna, however, noticed what had happened out of the corner of her eye.

"He tried to kick Michael!" she wailed.

"I tripped, my lady. It was an accident."

Ivan Tussler clenched his huge fists and gave Herbert such a ferocious stare that the paint began to peel off the door of one of the visitor's rooms.

"I'm sure no harm was done," said Sir Rudyard, spitting at Herbert when he said "sure".

Herbert was relieved once they were safely in their rooms. But just as he turned to go, he overheard them talking behind the door.

"Did you see it?" asked Sir Rudyard the Rancid's voice.

"Eet is ze beauty!" said Ivan Tussler.

"I want it *now*!" said Lady Belladonna.

"Patience, my dear," her husband was heard to reply. "All in good time." And there was burst of evil guffawing.

"I *knew* it!" said Herbert to himself as he went away. "There's definitely something fishy going on here."

·2·

One Feast – Many Headaches

That afternoon, before the feast, Herbert reported his findings to Sir Gadabout.

"I heard them talking about something being a 'beauty' and 'wanting' it. Sir Rudyard said, 'All in good time' in a very meaningful voice, sire."

"Don't always judge by appearances, Herbert. They may look like a rum lot, and not have quite the same ways as us, but that's probably because they come from a different country. We must be tolerant. They are lost, after all."

But Herbert wasn't satisfied. For once he applied his brain instead of his brawn, and before long had hit upon a plan. He didn't mention it to Sir Gadabout, just in case his master didn't approve. Instead, he finished his duties. He helped Sir Gadabout into his best clothes for the feast (Sir Gadabout's best blue shirt had yoghurt stains on one sleeve which

wouldn't come out. Herbert managed to hide them using a blue felt-tip pen). Finally, he put his master's teddy bear, Elvis, to bed with a hot water bottle, and then he was free to go.

Without hesitating, Herbert slipped out of Camelot and made his way to Merlin's cottage deep in Willow Wood. The very thought of the cottage made Herbert shudder. Merlin was King Arthur's great and terrible wizard: a tall, bony man with hypnotic blue eyes, a shock of grey hair and a beard to match. It was Merlin who had made Herbert invisible for the rescue

of Guinivere – not a pleasant experience, especially when he wanted to wipe his runny nose and couldn't even find it.

But it was not Merlin whom Herbert had come to visit; it was his grumpy, rude, but rather clever cat – Sidney Smith.

Herbert saw the old sign on Merlin's garden gate. It said:

BEWARE OF THE TURTLE

He didn't take too much notice of this. Last time, the suicidal guard-turtle had jumped at him from a tree and missed by miles. Herbert simply kept well clear of the trees and thought no more about it.

One thing that was different though was the door-knocker. It used to be a handle marked PULL which came out of the wall to reveal a hammer marked KNOCK. Now, the old sign saying PULL was attached to a piece of string lying on the ground. Herbert duly picked it up and gave it a tug. It soon became apparent that it was a long piece of string; it ran down the garden to a ramshackle old garage, and was attached to the garage door. When Herbert pulled it, the door flew open.

There was a mechanical spluttering sound, then the growl of a motorbike engine roaring into life. Suddenly, a turtle wearing a leather jacket, crash helmet and goggles, zoomed out of the garage on a little motorbike.

"ATTACK!" he yelled, with blood-curdling glee.

Herbert dived out of the way at the very last second, landing in Merlin's pond. The motorbike hit the doorstep at 75mph, catapulting its rider neatly through the letterbox.

The cottage door opened, and Sidney Smith, Merlin's ginger cat, unceremoniously deposited the dazed turtle on the doorstep. "Better luck next time, Dr McPherson." The unfortunate reptile limped dejectedly back to the garage, dragging his bent and lifeless machine and muttering, "Back to the drawing board."

When Sidney Smith saw Herbert dragging himself out of the pond, he raised an eyebrow snootily. "You rang?"

Herbert spat a newt out of his mouth and marched up to the smirking moggy, his shoes squelching loudly. "Why, I'll –"

"Now, now, brainless one. It's Merlin's idea, not mine."

Herbert remembered what he had come for, and with considerable effort, restrained himself. "I was just going to say how nice it is to see you again," he said, wringing the water from the bottom of his trousers.

"That must mean you're after something."

"Sort of. But it's not for me." Herbert went on to tell the cat about the strange visitors and his suspicions. "There's going to be a feast tonight in Rancid's honour. I thought it would be a good idea if you sized them up yourself — see if you can hear anything and keep a sharp eye out. I'm sure they're planning something."

Sidney Smith yawned. "Sorry, but I'm washing my whiskers tonight."

"I suppose," said Herbert craftily, using his brains rather than his brawn for the second time in one day, "that it would be too risky, what with Mad Mick the dog being there, and you only a cat . . ."

"Nonsense!" Sidney Smith spat, narrowing his green eyes.

"It's nothing to be ashamed of. He's not very big, but he is a fierce little brute. You're better off safe indoors."

"I'm not afraid of any dog-eared mongrel," protested Sidney Smith, testing his sharp claws

on Merlin's battered door. "Wait there while I fetch my umbrella. I'm coming to the feast."

As Herbert was a mere squire he was not invited to the feast. Only knights and their ladies could attend, although Ivan Tussler waited on Sir Rudyard the Rancid. The only knight who had had the nerve to object to Ivan Tussler in person had had all the hair singed off his head by one of the giant's murderous stares. (And had since only agreed to go to the feast if he could wear his helmet.)

Sidney Smith slipped into the Great Hall unnoticed. The long table was laden with food and drink of every description, and musicians played on their fiddles and pipes from the gallery above. King Arthur and Queen Guinivere sat at the head of the table, with Sir Rudyard the Rancid and Lady Belladonna on one side of them and Ivan Tussler in attendance. They were considerate enough to be seated near the roaring log fire, which meant that Sidney Smith would be able to curl up in

the warm whilst carrying out his spying duties.

But when he got there, he found to his utter disgust that someone else had got there before him. A sturdy little black dog sprawled in front of the fire on his back with his legs sticking in the air – Mad Mick. He was taking up the best spot as he slumbered contentedly, his legs twitching every now and then as he dreamed sweet dreams of nipping Knights of the Round Table in various places.

Sidney Smith crept up to the unsuspecting dog, lifted up the flap of one of its ears, took a deep breath, and yelled: "BATHTIME!" at the top of his voice. Mad Mick shot into the air with an ear-splitting scream, then hurtled out of the Great Hall without looking back. He was later seen quivering and whimpering under a table in the library.

Satisfied, Sidney Smith curled up in front of the fire and listened intently to the conversation between the King and his visitors. But as time passed, and nothing interesting was said, he had to struggle to stop himself from falling asleep.

Sir Rudyard was stuffing food into his mouth as if it were his last meal for a year. He spat crumbs over half the guests as he said things like, "Super sizzling sausages, sire!"

Lady Belladonna kept whining, "This tastes *horrid*. This isn't cooked properly!" then promptly shovelled whatever it was into her mouth in a most disgusting manner. Ivan Tussler was cracking coconuts open with his bare hands, and made short work of a whole roasted boar which had been meant to feed twenty-four people at least. King Arthur blinked in disbelief at all this, but was far too polite to say anything. Meanwhile, Sir Gadabout had accidentally bent his knife and was trying to straighten it out by sitting on it whilst no one was looking.

By now Sidney Smith was certain that Herbert's fears were all in his tiny mind and he was just about to nod off ... when something happened. He noticed Sir Rudyard wink at Ivan Tussler, who put down the mammoth-sized pie he was about to demolish and left the Great Hall. Soon, he returned carrying an enormous barrel, which he put down beside Sir Rudyard – again with a purposeful wink. Sir Rudyard the Rancid rose to his feet.

"Your Majesty, ladies and gentlemen," he announced. "Please join me in a drink of King Meliodas' special brew. It is the finest wine in Lyonnesse and we know he would like us to share it with you as a 'thank you' for your hospitality."

Sir Rudyard then began to fill goblets from the barrel and pass them down the table. Sidney Smith sprang to his feet, about to warn King Arthur that he was sure the drink contained something it wasn't supposed to. Before he could do anything, he heard a deep, extremely angry growl behind him. He turned just in time to see Mad Mick bounding to-

wards him with his sharp teeth bared. Sidney
Smith dodged to one side, and the dog ended
up taking a chunk out of the table leg.

The chase was on. Mad Mick was fast, but
Sidney Smith was nimble, and knew the
passages and corridors of Camelot like the
back of his paw. He led the snapping, barking
mutt a merry dance. Finally he got rid of him
by squeezing through a narrow gap behind a
bookcase. When Mad Mick attempted it, he

jammed his head fast with a yelp. Kick and struggle as he might, he could not get free. Sidney Smith wriggled out the other side and dashed back to the Great Hall.

He was too late. The entire company had just drunk a toast to King Meliodas. The drink, whatever it was, was beginning to take effect ...

King Arthur was doing handstands and whistling "Three Blind Mice", Queen Guinivere believed she was the fairy on the Christmas tree and was climbing a large rubber plant,

and Sir Gadabout was trying to persuade people that he had once discovered the Lost City of Atlantis in the back pocket of his gardening trousers. The rest of the Knights of the Round Table were behaving in a similarly silly fashion – and Sir Rudyard the Rancid, Lady Belladonna and Ivan Tussler had all disappeared.

And when morning came, it was soon discovered that something else had disappeared with them ...

·3·

Stolen!

Early next morning, Herbert rushed into Sir Gadabout's room.

"Sire, have you heard? Excalibur has been stolen!"

"Oh, my poor head," Sir Gadabout groaned. "What did you say?"

"King Arthur's Excalibur has disappeared. *He's* got a headache, too ..."

Sir Gadabout slowly got out of bed and began to dress. Any sudden movement made his throbbing head feel worse. "Let's go outside and get some fresh air," he said. "You can tell me all about it then."

On the way out, they came across Sidney Smith lapping up a saucer of milk.

"Have you heard about Excalibur?" cried Herbert. "It's been —"

"Stolen — I know," said the ginger cat between slurps. "That's not all I know."

"What do you mean?" asked Sir Gadabout.

"I know who stole it."

"Come outside with us," said Sir Gadabout,

rubbing his poor old head. "We're going for some fresh air."

As soon as they set foot outside, Sir Gadabout pressed his hands to his ears. "Ouch! Who's making all that noise?"

There was a lot of banging and clanging coming from behind the stables.

When they went to investigate, they stumbled upon Sir Rudyard the Rancid and his party. They were packed, ready to leave, but Sir Rudyard appeared to be practising with his sword. Ivan Tussler uprooted a thirty-foot oak tree as if it were a weed, and held it out at arm's length. Sir Rudyard swung his sword – and sliced through the tree trunk in one go.

"Fantastic!" he exclaimed.

Then, Ivan Tussler took the sword – it looked like a kitchen knife in his fist – and attacked a large granite boulder, chopping it up like a diced carrot.

"Ze blade – she is not even marked," commented Ivan.

"Wait a minute," said Sir Gadabout.

"That's Excalibur!" cried Herbert.

"That's what I was trying to tell you," said Sidney Smith.

Sir Rudyard wiped his greasy mouth with the back of his hand, and blinked the little piggy eyes in his potato head. "Two fools and

a cat trying to tell me that my own sword, known as ... umm ... the Fearless Flasher, which I've owned and cleaned and polished for forty years, is King Arthur's renowned Excalibur?"

Sir Gadabout knew very well that it *was* Excalibur, but since Sir Rudyard was the King's guest, it was a delicate matter, and he could hardly start making such serious accusations until he had definite proof.

"We were merely observing that there is a certain similarity –"

"He's calling you a liar!" screeched Lady Belladonna, her pointed nose positively quivering with rage.

"I assure you, my Lady –"

"Now he's calling *me* a liar!" she wailed, tears suddenly pouring in floods down her face.

"How DARE you?" roared Sir Rudyard.

"Oh dear," groaned Sir Gadabout. He went to offer his handkerchief to the weeping Lady Belladonna.

"Look out, Ruddy!" she cried. "He's going to kill us! Chop his head off with Excal– with the Fearless Flasher!"

"Monstrous!" growled Sir Rudyard, his little fat cheeks wobbling with indignation. "Sir, you offend my eyes. I must ask my squire to escort you from my presence."

The ground rumbled as Ivan Tussler stomped towards Sir Gadabout and his loyal companions.

"There seems to have been a misunderstanding – and I must warn Mr Tussler that I am a knight, trained in the arts of combat and – YEAARGH!"

Sir Gadabout's voice became muffled as the giant gathered the three of them up in one go. It was a bit like making bread, really. He

rubbed them, he pummelled them, he kneaded them and rolled them around until they formed a dough of armour, clothes and ginger fur. But instead of putting them in the oven, he rolled them like a bowling ball back the way they'd come. They only eventually came to a halt by crashing into some milk churns which went flying like skittles. Meanwhile, Sir Rudyard and his party hurried off in a cloud of dust.

Sir Gadabout, Herbert and Sidney Smith managed to unravel and dust themselves down.

"Did you see that mad dog laughing?" spat an outraged Sidney Smith.

"I'd like to take that Tussler on in a *fair* fight," muttered Herbert, smoothing his ruffled hair.

"Isn't one against three fair enough for you?" taunted Sidney Smith.

Sidney Smith then proceeded to tell them everything he had seen the previous night.

"We must report to King Arthur immediately," said Sir Gadabout.

"Let's see how that Tussler can handle an army of Knights of the Round Table!" said Herbert. "Mind you, I could have sorted him out myself if he hadn't taken me by surprise. I'm taller than I look."

"There's a fat chance of getting an army together," said Sidney Smith. "The King's lying down in a darkened room and refuses to be disturbed, and Lancelot and the others have got even *worse* hangovers. They're not capable of lifting a spoonful of cornflakes, let alone a sword. *We* must go after Mad Mick – I mean Excalibur – by ourselves."

"I'm not sure *I'm* capable of lifting a sword," groaned Sir Gadabout.

"But the difference is," pointed out Sidney Smith, "you never were, so it won't matter. Besides, you've got me."

Herbert rounded on the cat for insulting his master, but Sir Gadabout intervened. "He's right. We must go after Excalibur without delay. Saddle up Pegasus – quietly." Pegasus was Sir Gadabout's horse – a knock-kneed bag of bones whom he had rescued from a retirement stable because he felt sorry for him.

Within minutes they were off, but progress was slow. Every time Pegasus put a hoof down, Sir Gadabout felt as if he were being hit on the head with a hammer. "Ooh! ... Ow! ... Ooh!" Sidney Smith got a free ride in Herbert's saddlebag, and was not at all sympathetic to Sir Gadabout's fragile state.

There weren't many paths leading from Camelot's gates, and at first it was easy for

them to decide which way to go. Every so often they would see someone hopping about with teeth-marks in his ankle, or busily bandaging a hand – and they knew that Mad Mick could not be far ahead.

But the further they got from Camelot, the harder it became for them to follow the trail. The last clue they found was a cat clinging to the very top branch of a tree, its fur standing on end, its eyes wide with fear and shock, and its teeth chattering so much it couldn't speak.

Just when they had to come to a decision

about which way to go next, they saw a cottage ahead of them.

"We could ask there," suggested Sir Gadabout.

"Don't you recognize it?" said Sidney Smith, who of course had very good eyesight.

"It – it does look rather familiar ..."

It was a red cottage with an unusually tall chimney.

"Blow me down," Herbert exclaimed. "It's Morag's cottage!"

Morag was the witch who, with her sister

Demelza, had kidnapped Guinivere. Sir Gadabout pulled down the visor of his helmet. The last time he had been here he had had some rather smelly and unpleasant substances poured over him.

"Er, I'm sure she won't know anything about it," he said feebly.

"There's a sign on the cottage door," Sidney Smith said. "Let's at least see what it says."

So they went to the cottage and looked at the wooden sign nailed to the door.

"I hope that means solving them," commented Sir Gadabout uneasily.

"This is just what we need, sire — detectives."

"This is the last thing we need," said Sidney Smith acidly.

"I suppose it's worth a try—what else can we do?" said Sir Gadabout, and he knocked on the door.

·4·

Morag and Demelza

It was opened by a woman with long black hair, a great hook-nose and a jutting chin.

"Ah!" Demelza exclaimed. "The great Sir Gadabout and his friends. Do not look so worried – my sister and I have given up our witching ways. Detective work is an honest and caring profession – and there is, ahem, more money in it."

"I see," said Sir Gadabout, not entirely convinced. "Well, I've come about –"

"We know what you've come about! My sister's powers of deduction have already been at work; she awaits you in her consulting room."

"Ooh," said Herbert as they followed Demelza. "Perhaps they really *are* detectives now." They passed a framed newspaper-cutting on the wall which said, "MORAG SOLVES THE MYSTERY OF THE MAN WITH THE BLUE NOSE – Great Sleuth says 'I knew he'd blow it'."

And although from a distance the name "Morag" seemed to have been written on a

piece of paper and stuck over something else, Sir Gadabout thought this might simply be due to a printing error, and was very impressed. He was left in no doubt when he noticed something else on the wall. Next to the door which Demelza was just opening was a framed diploma: "This is to certify that Morag Broomspell studied for her degree in Detective Skills on 12 November and passed her exam on 13 November. Signed 'Nosher' Clegg, Postal School of Detection, Acupuncture and Archery, Wapping."

Morag was standing by the fireplace when they went into the room. She was taller than Demelza, with long grey hair. She wore her usual ragged dress made out of an old sack, but on her head she wore a deerstalker – the sort of hat worn by Sherlock Holmes. She was puffing thoughtfully on the old pipe they all remembered only too well, and when they drew closer to her, she blew some foul-smelling green smoke into their faces. It was so awful that Sidney Smith's whiskers wilted. Morag held the pipe in one hand; her other was in her pocket as she leaned nonchalantly against the mantelpiece.

"Let me see," she began, looking them up and down. "You have come on horseback. You are seeking two . . . no, three people and a dog. I deduce that there are two men: a fat, disgusting one and a huge, muscular one. There is also a woman – she is thin and nasty. Now, I suspect that the dog is not big, but very cunning and with long, sharp teeth."

"Amazing!" cried Sir Gadabout.

"How could you possibly work all that out just by looking at us?"

"I have my methods," she said serenely.

"Show us your hand," demanded Sidney Smith.

Morag reluctantly revealed her hand – wrapped in a very thick, bloodstained bandage. "They passed this way an hour ago," she owned up grumpily. "But I could have deduced all that even if they hadn't – by looking at the colour of the mud on your boots, and, er, whether you've got a limp and all that sort of thing."

"Remarkable!" said Sir Gadabout, his admiration undiminished.

"We nearly turned the beastly thing into a toothless poodle with pink ribbons . . ." began Demelza.

"But we don't do that sort of thing now," added Morag hastily.

"Blow!" moaned Sidney Smith. "They go all honest on you just when you need them."

"Ah!" said Demelza. "But we can help you in another way. My sister, using her unrivalled detecting abilities, can tell you where to look for them."

"Elementary, my dear Demelza. The case of the Fat Fiend and his Demented Dog is most

singular indeed. Having studied numerous cigarette ends, footprints and cloud formations, I suggest that you proceed two furlongs north by north-east, to the Sign of the Crown."

"Down the road to the pub," Demelza translated.

"Then, many leagues west to the Seventh Convergence, where I recall solving the Case of the Hound of the Braithwaites ..."

"Down the M5 Packhorse Road and take Junction Seven," explained Demelza. "She found her aunt's Yorkshire Terrier there last week."

"After this, you must seek out a tall, dark stranger with a long pointed hat."

"A witch!" cried Herbert.

"No," said Demelza. "A policeman – to ask the way. From then on you will be in the remotest part of Lyonnesse, where the fog never lifts and the only sound is that of howling wolves. Many of the boldest and bravest have travelled there – never to be seen again. And *that* is where Sir Rudyard the Rancid's castle lies."

For a moment, they thought they heard someone working furiously at a typewriter in another room – but then they discovered that it was Sir Gadabout's teeth chattering.

"A little c-cold in here, isn't it?" he re-marked unconvincingly.

Morag clapped a hand to her head and collapsed into a chair. "Now I am exhausted by this brilliant deduction. Demelza, fetch me my violin."

"Just think how tired you'd be if they hadn't *told* you where they were going," said Sidney Smith sarcastically.

Sir Gadabout hastily thanked Morag and Demelza and bade them farewell. He had just

reached the door when Morag, making a remarkable recovery, bounded out of her chair and blocked his path.

"Glad to be of service. I think you will find that my fees are very reasonable."

"What ... er ... oh, of course." And Herbert, who carried Sir Gadabout's money, had to fork out a tidy sum before they were on their way once more.

They followed the path to the pub and then on to the M5 Packhorse Road, but it took them

two whole days to reach Junction Seven. And the weather changed dramatically as soon as they left the main road. They rode out of warm sunshine into thick, damp fog, so dense they could only see a few feet in front of them. The dampness went straight to poor old Pegasus' chest, and made him cough so much he sounded more like a donkey. Wolves howled, and there were mysterious rustlings going on in the trees and bushes all around them. They had the distinct feeling that they were being watched.

Then suddenly, through the gloom, they saw a black shape lying on the path ahead. At first, it looked like a bundle of rags, but as they got closer they could see that it was a dog. And when they got closer still, they recognized ... Mad Mick.

He was flat on his back, hardly able to move a muscle, and whimpering like a baby. It was a pitiful sight.

"He's been attacked by wolves," said Herbert.

"If they can do that to *him*," gulped Sir Gadabout, "what's going to become of us?"

·5·

Castle Rancid

"Let's leave him," said Herbert, remembering his master's bitten hand.

"We can't do that," said Sidney Smith to everyone's surprise – but then he added, "Let's put him out of his misery!"

"A Knight of the Round Table has a duty to help anyone or anything in distress," said Sir Gadabout. He went to have a look at the stricken dog, and Mad Mick managed to find the strength to wag his limp tail.

"There, there, old chap," said Sir Gadabout, stroking Mad Mick's head. The dog let out a little whine. "He's covered in blood, poor creature."

Sidney Smith lifted his nose into the air. "Smells more like –"

"YEEAAARGH!" said Sir Gadabout as Mad Mick sprang up and clamped his vicious yellow teeth into the knight's nose.

"– tomato sauce," continued Sidney Smith.

Sir Gadabout was bellowing, hopping and twisting, trying to shake the beast free. "I CAHD GET HIB OFF BY DOSE!"

Fists flailed and fur flew as Herbert and Sidney Smith joined in the fray. Unfortunately, such was their enthusiasm that they did more harm to Sir Gadabout than to the grimly clinging Mad Mick.

"Dot be – hib!" cried Sir Gadabout, the sharp teeth bringing tears to his eyes.

Eventually, Herbert and Sidney Smith's efforts bore fruit, and Mad Mick had to let go. He scampered away, laughing, into the fog.

"What a mess he's made of your hooter," Sidney Smith commented. And indeed, Sir Gadabout's throbbing nose was looking rather like a grated beetroot.

"I'll attend to it, sire," Herbert said, fetching the first aid kit he always carried with him. He put some ointment on his master's painful nose, then wrapped a little bandage round it.

"At least," Sir Gadabout said when he had finally recovered from the shock, "this means we can't be too far from Sir Rudyard's castle."

They continued, slowly and cautiously, along the same murky, shivery-cold path, trying to ignore the menacing cry of the wolves and the flapping bats.

After about an hour, Sidney Smith suddenly said, "Can you smell that?"

"No," said Herbert.

"I can't sbell *eddythig*," moaned Sir Gadabout.

"It's a nasty smell. Sort of . . . rancid!"

Forewarned, they dismounted, tethered their horses, and advanced on foot. And just around the next bend in the path, their eyes fell on the dreaded place itself – Castle Rancid.

It was an ugly, gloomy, sinister building. Vultures flew overhead, and skeletons could be seen scattered around the foot of its massive, forbidding walls. The hair on Sir Gadabout's head stood on end with such force that his helmet flew into the air and was caught expertly by Herbert.

"Look," said Sidney Smith. He was pointing at a little group of people outside the castle walls – it was Sir Rudyard the Rancid and his crowd.

"I'm going to get closer to find out what they're up to," announced Sidney Smith. And he crept away, scraping his tummy along the grass the way he did when he was stalking birds. Finally, he hid behind a bush near to where Sir Rudyard's crew had gathered.

He saw that they were lolling around a huge picnic hamper. Sir Rudyard was leaning his great bulk against it and eating boiled eggs without bothering to remove the shells, and Lady Belladonna was sucking the insides out of old, blackened bananas (which was the only way she would eat them).

Sir Rudyard finished the last egg with a crunch and started on a large trout – he liked to eat the eyes first, then nibble the scales off. It made Sidney Smith's mouth water.

"Tussler," said Sir Rudyard, bits of fish flying in all directions, "that Gadabit will be here soon – unless Mad Mick has frightened him off. Our little plan will work, won't it?"

"Ze plan – she is full of wonder!"

Sidney Smith's ears pricked up. What plan was this? He decided he had to see what the giant was up to. He seemed to be hunched over Sir Rudyard's shield and spear, busily doing something to them. Whatever it was, the shrewd cat knew that it must be some sort of trickery in case Sir Gadabout should challenge him to a joust. Sidney Smith doubted whether this lazy slob could beat even Sir Gadabout in a fair joust. But what sort of chicanery was he up to?

Mad Mick was lying contentedly on his belly gnawing a large bone (which looked suspiciously like a human thigh-bone). Sidney

Smith wanted to climb a little pear tree nearby which would give him a view of what Ivan Tussler was up to, but he knew dogs had such good hearing that if he made the slightest sound the savage beast would hear.

However, Sidney Smith was nothing if not confident, and he decided to try it. He inched up to the tree, then using his sharp claws he scampered right up the trunk and settled into one of the branches. Perfect – he hadn't even heard himself! Now, he would be able to see what Ivan was about.

But he had forgotten one thing – it is not only hearing that dogs are good at.

Mad Mick stopped gnawing the bone and

began to sniff. He sniffed to the north, he sniffed to the south, the east and the west. The hairs on the back of his neck bristled. He stood up, sniffing again, and turned towards the pear tree.

Sidney Smith cursed his back luck. He knew that the stupid dog couldn't get at him whilst he was up the tree – but once he had sounded the alarm, Ivan Tussler was tall enough to reach up and grab him. There was only one thing for it. Giving up all pretence of keeping quiet, he leapt from the branch and ran as fast as he could.

He could hear Mad Mick snarling and snapping after him. Sidney Smith actually felt a surge of panic. He would never be able to make it back to his companions in time – and what help would they be anyway?

He took a risk and veered off the path into the dense, dark forest. Almost immediately, he was confronted by a pair of bright, evil, yellow eyes. A wolf. He turned to his right, only to see another pair of glinting eyes. Every way he turned, he found himself staring into narrow, unblinking wolf-eyes. He was surrounded.

Sidney Smith hadn't spent years as a wizard's companion for nothing. He had an idea. Under Merlin's tuition he had learned not

only to talk to humans, but to converse in many animal languages. In his best Wolf, he said, "Phew, I've been looking for you boys everywhere. It's that Mad Mick from Castle Rancid. He says this forest isn't big enough for you and him – and he's going to kick you out. He's on his way right now. I know there's a lot of you, and I'm sure you're very brave, but he *has* got these big yellow teeth and –"

Just then, Mad Mick hurtled into the circle of wolves. Jaws snapped and fur flew – but

none of it was ginger. Sidney Smith scampered away in the direction of Sir Gadabout and Herbert.

He had not gone fifty paces when he heard a low, deep growl from above. Looking up, he saw Mad Mick in the branch of a tree just ahead where he had been tossed by the wolves, who were disgusted by his rancid smell and his tough skin. Mick's tail and ears were chewed in half, and he was covered in ragged bald patches. With a roar, he sprang at Sidney Smith.

But the cat had had time to collect his wits. "Dr McPherson could do better than that,"

remarked Sidney Smith calmly as he stepped aside. Like a matador, he held out his bag which contained a lot of loose change and other bits and bobs. Just before he thudded to the ground, Mad Mick's jaws snapped shut on the bag. There was a painful gulp, and the dog started to look distinctly seasick. He limped away, and there was a jingle of coins from his belly every time he put a paw down.

Sidney Smith grinned and quickly reported his triumph to his companions.

·6·

Sir Rudyard's Secret Weapon

"What on earth can they be up to?" Sir Gadabout wondered.

"He knows we're after him," said Sidney Smith. "He must have some kind of plot to make sure he beats you in a joust – that way, King Arthur could no longer claim Excalibur back, because Rancid could say he had won the right to it in a fair fight."

"Then I must find out exactly what they're doing," said Sir Gadabout.

"I'll come with you, sire," said the faithful squire.

"I knew you would." Sir Gadabout gave him a friendly pat on the back. They both hurried out to where Sidney Smith had told them Sir Rudyard was. But now Mad Mick was on guard, prowling up and down, sniffing the air, and swivelling his ears in all directions. Every now and then he would let out a ferocious bark, just in case anyone he hadn't spotted might think he *had* seen them. It was a dangerous thing to make a fool of Mad Mick – it was even more dangerous to do so if you were a cat. To make things worse, eating Sidney Smith's bag had given the desperate dog hiccups, which were making him jingle like a toy money-box.

"This seems to be a rather tricky situation," assessed Sir Gadabout.

"Leave it to me, sire," said Herbert. From his bag he produced a juicy steak which had been intended for their next meal. He attached it to a long piece of string, then climbed the same tree that Sidney Smith had been stuck in. Next, he threw the delicious-smelling meat in the direction of Mad Mick.

The dog stopped prowling, lifted his nose in the air, and began sniffing frantically. Inch by inch he edged towards the steak, although he could not see it lying in the long grass. And every time the dog got closer, Herbert pulled the steak a little further away.

"Off you go, sire," whispered Herbert.

"Eh?" said Sir Gadabout. "Oh – I see!" He crept up to the bushes and positioned himself so that he could get a glimpse of Ivan Tussler and Sir Rudyard. Sir Rudyard was still slouched against the picnic hamper. He was shoving plums into his mouth six pounds at a

time, and crunching and grinding the stones
with his teeth. Ivan Tussler was doing *something* to Sir Rudyard's spear and shield, but he
was doing it very secretively, and Sir
Gadabout just couldn't get a proper look. That
was soon to change.

Mad Mick was by this time right under the
tree in which Herbert was hiding. Herbert was
dangling the steak in the air, making the dog
jump for it. He knew he couldn't keep this

game up for ever, but he was hoping to tire Mick out before letting him eat the steak.

Suddenly, Ivan Tussler got to his feet. "Ze spear and ze shield – she is ready."

"Right," said Sir Rudyard. "Good work, Tussler. Let's try it out." Slowly, and with a great deal of effort, he hoisted himself upright.

"Ze spear first." Ivan Tussler handed his master the spear he had been furtively tampering with. Sir Gadabout noticed that the tip of the spear, which should have been a sharp, shiny point, was black and round, as if some kind of ball were on the end.

"We'll pretend I'm on my horse," said Sir Rudyard, "and that big boulder over there is Sir Gadalot. Here we go."

He broke into a shambling run, immediately began to puff and pant and slowed to an unsteady jog, then ground to a halt six feet from the boulder, red-faced and gasping for air. He handed the spear to Ivan. "Here ... you do it ..." he wheezed.

The big man took the spear and jabbed it against the boulder. The strange spear-tip exploded, and when the smoke had cleared, the rock lay shattered in tiny fragments.

"Got him!" cried Lady Belladonna with glee.

"Oh dear," Sir Gadabout whispered to himself.

"And now, the shield," commanded Sir Rudyard. "I'll hold it, Tussler, and you come at me with a normal spear."

He planted his feet firmly on the ground and held the shield out at chest height. Sir Gadabout noticed that it had wires hanging out of the bottom. Ivan Tussler advanced on his master carrying another spear, and thrust it against the shield. There was a loud BOING! and the centre portion of the shield shot out on a spring, sending Ivan Tussler sailing backwards through the air.

Sir Gadabout felt rather faint.

Ivan Tussler landed on the branch next to Herbert. Herbert screamed, the branch broke, and he suddenly plummeted to the ground and found himself sitting on a sore bottom, staring Mad Mick in the face. Sir Gadabout rushed to his squire's assistance, but before any blood was spilled, Sir Rudyard's voice was heard bellowing:

"GADALOT! I take it that you and your foolish friends have come to steal my sword, which I've cared for like a son for fifty years and more?"

"That sword is Excalibur, and belongs to King Arthur," said Sir Gadabout trying to sound brave. "I hereby challenge you to a joust so that I can win the sword back for my King."

"I see. Er, you *are* the twit known as Sir Gadalot – the fumbling, stumbling, grumbling walking disaster in armour?"

"I wouldn't say he was 'grumbling'," said Sidney Smith, and got a clip round the ear from Herbert.

"My name is Sir Gadabout."

"Good. Then we shall fight like true knights over Excal– I mean the Fearless Flasher, at dawn!"

·7·

Sir Gadabout Faces the Music

After a cold, scary night camped outside Castle Rancid, Sir Gadabout rose while it was still dark and was helped into his armour by Herbert.

"What am I to do? I'm the King's only hope; I must get Excalibur back, yet I'm up against exploding spears and rebounding shields."

"Don't worry, sire," said Herbert. "I talked to Sidney Smith last night, and we came up with a plan ..."

A huge crowd had gathered for the joust – there were even a few people there to support Sir Gadabout, and he guessed they were folk who had suffered at the hands of Sir Rudyard. Although the rest of the crowd was baying for Sir Gadabout's blood, Ivan Tussler could be seen approaching each person individually wielding a big stick. As soon as they started shouting "Kill the Clown from Camelot!" and suchlike, Tussler would give them five pence

and move on to the next person. An announcer
from Castle Rancid shouted, "Five minutes to
tilt-off," through a loudhailer. "May the best
man win, and failing that, may Sir Gadalot
win."

Herbert and Sidney Smith approached Sir
Gadabout.

"You look a little ... fatter," Sir Gadabout
commented when he saw the cat.

"I had a big fish supper," Sidney Smith
replied, winking at Herbert. And then they did

a strange thing. Without another word to Sir
Gadabout, they both hurried off to Sir
Rudyard's end of the field.

"Hang on – you're supposed to get *me*
ready!" cried Sir Gadabout, aghast.

"We'll be back shortly, sire," shouted
Herbert.

The two plotters scampered over to where
Ivan Tussler was lowering Sir Rudyard on to
his horse. The odious knight glared at them
and called, "MICK!"

He appeared from nowhere, eyes red with anger, and yellow teeth bared viciously. He ignored Herbert and bounded straight at Sidney Smith. The rather fatter-than-usual cat simply stood there mewing helplessly. The dog's mouth opened wider – he couldn't believe his luck. SNAP! His jaws encircled Sidney Smith's body as if to bite him com-

pletely in half. CLANG! The razor-sharp teeth bit into the cat's special armour, covered in ginger fur. In the night, he had obtained a piece of armour lying beside one of the skeletons outside Castle Rancid. Herbert had given him a close cut with a sharp pair of scissors and the resulting pile of fur had been stuck on to the armour. Sidney Smith chuckled cruelly as Mad Mick rolled on to his back whimpering and spitting teeth out left, right and centre.

Meanwhile, Herbert approached Ivan Tussler, who was preparing to hand over Sir Rudyard's shield. The top of his head came up to the giant's waist.

"Ever seen one of these?" asked Herbert, holding out a closed hand with great care, as if something precious were hidden inside.

The big man lowered his shaven head and peered at Herbert's fist, and Herbert let go the hardest upper-cut he had ever thrown in his life. The force of the punch landing on Ivan Tussler's jaw sent a pain all the way along Herbert's arm and down to his boots, making his laces come undone. For a moment, Ivan stood there as if nothing had happened. Herbert began to quake – his best-ever punch had had no effect! The plan was not going according to plan!

Then, the giant looked up at the sky. "I see

ze stars, please!" He keeled over like a felled tree and was lost in a cloud of dust.

Herbert stood staring at his fist. "I did it!"

"Come on!" cried Sidney Smith.

"I've always said I'm stronger than I look," said Herbert, as they ran back to Sir Gadabout.

"Where have you been?"

"Here's your spear and shield, sire."

"That's not my shield . . ."

"Off you go, sire."

"But –"

"LET THE JOUST COMMENCE!" cried the announcer.

"I'm going to be blown up!" cried Sir Gadabout as Pegasus ambled off.

Sir Rudyard kicked his horse with his spurs. There was an evil glint in his eye. "Excalibur will be *mine*! CHARGE!"

There was a thunder of hooves, and the two knights clashed. It has to be said that Sir Gadabout closed his eyes and screamed, and his spear missed Sir Rudyard by miles. Sir Rudyard's spear slammed into Sir Gadabout's shield – except of course, that it wasn't really Sir Gadabout's shield. The exploding spear met the rebounding shield with dire consequences. There was a BOOM! and a puff of smoke, and Sir Rudyard was seen rocketing into the air, getting smaller and smaller, and

heading in the general direction of Budapest. Excalibur fell out of his scabbard and landed behind a hedge next to the jousting field. Sir Gadabout's face was blackened and his armour smoking, but he was otherwise unharmed. He scurried off to retrieve the bejewelled sword.

He, Herbert and Sidney Smith made their getaway during the ensuing chaos, bearing

King Arthur's precious sword back to
Camelot.

There, they were treated like heroes, and
showered with kisses from Queen Guinivere
("He *has* missed it," she told them), and
handshakes and pats on the back from King
Arthur. Sidney Smith made sure everyone saw
his cunning piece of armour, complete with

Mad Mick's teeth marks; Herbert proudly told the story of how he had laid low the Man Mountain.

"Actually," he said, "my muscles look as big as his if I fold my arms like this . . ."

Sir Gadabout was being very modest about his victory. "It's really just a matter of taking aim early and keeping a steady nerve . . ."

And if everyone knew deep down that Sir Gadabout was still the Worst Knight in the World, it was quite a while before they mentioned it again.